THE LAST PUPPY

The Last Puppy

FRANK ASCH

LITTLE SIMON
Published by Simon & Schuster Inc., New York

Special thanks to Sue Thompson

Copyright © 1980 by Frank Asch
All rights reserved including the right of reproduction
in whole or in part in any form.
Published by Simon and Schuster Books for Young Readers
A Division of Simon & Schuster, Inc.
Simon & Schuster Building
Rockefeller Center
1230 Avenue of the Americas
New York, NY 10020

Simon and Schuster Books for Young Readers
is a trademark of Simon & Schuster, Inc.
Manufactured in the United States of America.

10   9   8   7   6   5   4

10   9   8   7   6   5   4   3   (pbk.)

Library of Congress Cataloging in Publication Data
Asch, Frank. The last puppy.
SUMMARY: The last born of nine puppies worries that
he will be the last chosen for a pet of a new owner.
[1. Dogs—Fiction. I. Title. PZ7.A778Las [E] 80-215
ISBN 0-671-66276-7
ISBN 0-671-66687-8 (pbk.)

To Winnie and Gesso

I was the last of Momma's nine puppies.

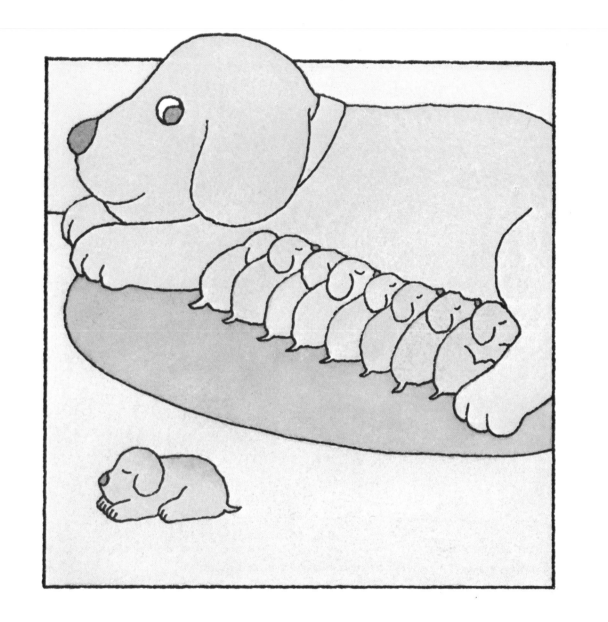

The last to eat from Momma,
the last to open my eyes,

the last to learn to drink milk
from a saucer,

and the last one into the doghouse
at night.

I was the last puppy.

One day Momma's owner put up a sign:
PUPPIES FOR SALE.

The next day, a little girl came
and took one of us away.
That night I couldn't sleep very well.
I kept wondering:
When will my turn come?
Will I be the last puppy again?

In the morning, a little boy
came to choose a puppy.
"Take me, Take me!" I barked.
"That puppy's too noisy," he said,
and picked another puppy instead.

Later that day, a nice lady from
the city almost picked me.
But when I tried to jump into
her lap, she fell backwards
right into our bowl of milk.

When a farmer and his family
came to choose a puppy,
I got so excited when
the farmer picked me up,
I bit him on the nose.
They picked two puppies,
leaving four of us behind.

Soon there were just three of us left.

Then two,

then just me, the last puppy.

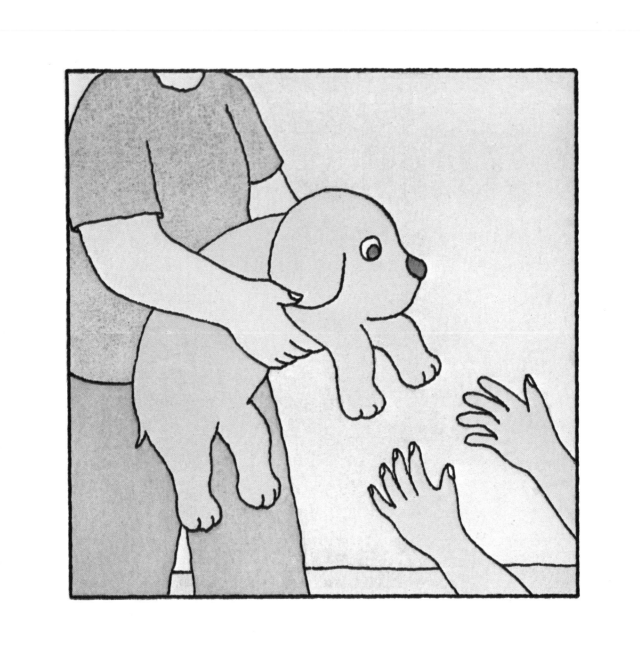

But one day, my turn came, too.
Big hands picked me up
and gave me to a little boy.
We got into a car
and drove away.

The little boy held me on his lap.
He put his face down close to mine
and I licked him on the nose.

He laughed and said,
"You know what?
You're my first puppy."